The Adventures of Theseus and His Friends

Aegean Sea

Athens

Icaria

Naxos

Minos' palace

Theseus' road to Athens:
· · · · · · · · · ·

Theseus' journey to King Minos'
palace on Crete and his return:

Daedalus' and Icarus' escape
from King Minos and Crete:
- - - - - - - - →

N
W · E
S

ROBERT BYRD

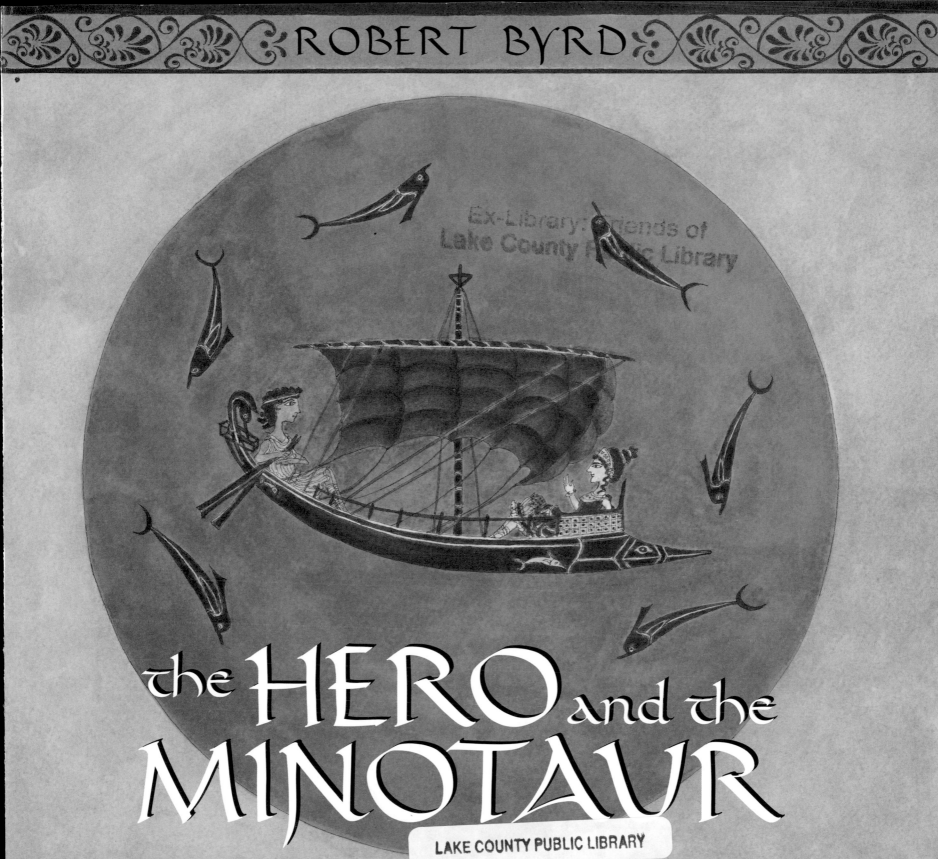

the HERO and the MINOTAUR

The Fantastic Adventures of Theseus

Dutton Children's Books ✶ New York

To my son, Rob

DUTTON CHILDREN'S BOOKS
A division of Penguin Young Readers Group
Published by the Penguin Group • Penguin Group (USA) Inc., 375 Hudson Street, New York, New York 10014, U.S.A.
Penguin Group (Canada), 10 Alcorn Avenue, Toronto, Ontario, Canada M4V 3B2 (a division of Pearson Penguin Canada Inc.)
Penguin Books Ltd, 80 Strand, London WC2R 0RL, England
Penguin Ireland, 25 St Stephen's Green, Dublin 2, Ireland (a division of Penguin Books Ltd)
Penguin Group (Australia), 250 Camberwell Road, Camberwell, Victoria 3124, Australia (a division of Pearson Australia Group Pty Ltd)
Penguin Books India Pvt Ltd, 11 Community Centre, Panchsheel Park, New Delhi - 110 017, India
Penguin Group (NZ), Cnr Airborne and Rosedale Roads, Albany, Auckland 1310, New Zealand (a division of Pearson New Zealand Ltd)
Penguin Books (South Africa) (Pty) Ltd, 24 Sturdee Avenue, Rosebank, Johannesburg 2196, South Africa
Penguin Books Ltd, Registered Offices: 80 Strand, London WC2R 0RL, England

CIP Data is available.

Published in the United States by Dutton Children's Books,
a division of Penguin Young Readers Group
345 Hudson Street, New York, New York 10014
www.penguin.com/youngreaders

Designed by Beth Herzog and Sara Reynolds

Manufactured in China
ISBN 0-525-47391-2

First Edition

1 3 5 7 9 10 8 6 4 2

Ages ago, in the days of gods and monsters, mighty Poseidon ruled the seas. This fearsome god rode over the waters in a golden chariot, forming earthquakes, furious storms, and thunderous waves in his wake. Yet he also drove the joyful dolphins, brought calm winds for smooth sailing, and created all of the delights of the sparkling ocean. Poseidon's brother was Zeus, king of all the gods.

In those days the gods mixed freely in the affairs of humankind. They even let themselves feel human emotions — jealousy, anger, envy, and love — for men and women on Earth. Poseidon loved a woman, the beautiful Princess Aethra of Troezen, and watched over her tenderly. When Aethra fell in love with a human king and gave birth to a son, Theseus, Poseidon protected him . . . but that is getting ahead of the story.

Poseidon was called the earth-shaker, for once long ago he shook his mighty trident, and the oceans churned and roared before him. The goddess of the moon, the god of the sun, and all the ancient spirits looked on in awe as earth rose up from the bottom of the sea and the glorious lands of Greece were born. The most beautiful countryside was filled with craggy mountains and green olive groves, watered by clear streams and warmed by a bright sun. King Aegeus ruled there from the city of Athens. Aegeus was a good king, but there were many who were jealous of his power and threatened him. So when the king traveled to Troezen, met Princess Aethra, and had a son with her, the mother and baby stayed safely in that town, while he returned to Athens.

In Troezen, inspired by his mother's tales of great heroes and warriors, Theseus grew to be strong and brave. When he was only seven, Heracles, the greatest hero of Greece, walked into the city wearing the skin of a lion. Theseus' friends mistook Heracles for a lion walking on its hind legs and fled in terror. But Theseus grabbed an ax and advanced, determined to slay the beast. The boy's bravery delighted Heracles, and the two became friends. Theseus soon vowed to become a hero like Heracles. While Heracles relied on his awesome strength, Theseus was clever, quick, and developed his wrestling skills.

Theseus often questioned his mother about his father. "Who is he? When can I go to him?" he would ask. His mother always answered that she would tell him when the time was right.

One morning, in a part of the forest where the trees grew thickly on either side of the path, Theseus came upon an enormous boulder blocking his way. He strained against it with all his might, and slowly it began to move. Beneath it Theseus found a pair of golden sandals and a shining golden sword.

Aethra recognized what Theseus had found and said to him, "Your father, King Aegeus, left these treasures here for you. 'When our son is strong enough to turn the rock,' he told me, 'he must put on the sandals, take up the sword, and come to me in Athens. I shall recognize him by these things.'" Theseus was overjoyed to learn about his father. He wondered what it would be like to meet the great king.

Aethra helped Theseus prepare for his journey, though she was sad to see him leave Troezen and anxious for his safety. "You must take the sea route to Athens," she said, "for the road is filled with robbers and monsters."

But talk of danger only filled Theseus with excitement. Hoping to prove his courage, he decided to travel by land in spite of his mother's warning. So he set off along the road for Athens, his father's sandals on his feet and the golden sword strapped to his side.

Though the rocky path wound among desolate green hills and through rugged, lonely forests, Theseus felt only the thrill of adventure as he made his way to meet his father. After walking for some hours, he came upon a massive strongman named Cercyon, who liked to challenge travelers to a wrestling match and crush them to death. "Come, boy," Cercyon bellowed. "See if you can best me!" When Cercyon tried to grab him, Theseus was too clever for his tricks, and he nimbly stepped aside, causing Cercyon to stumble and lose his balance. Then Theseus, an accomplished wrestler, pressed the advantage and flipped the robber upside down. The evil grappler landed on his head and perished.

Next Theseus met Sinis the pine-bender, who was so tough he could bend pine trees down to the earth. Sinis would make travelers take hold of the treetop and then, letting go the tree, fling his victims to their doom. But Theseus proved too smart to be caught in that trap, and he made sure the pine-bender came to the very same end that he had brought to so many others.

As Poseidon watched from the sea, Theseus followed the road up and up along steep cliffs rising from the ocean below. At the top stood an enormous ogre called Sciron, who ordered all who passed to wash his feet. When they bent to the task, the ogre would kick the travelers into the sea, where a monstrous turtle waited to devour them. "I will wash your feet, sir, but first I must clean the water," Theseus called out to the ogre. "See how dirty it is?" When Sciron leaned down to look, Theseus quickly crashed the bowl over the giant's head and kicked him over the cliff. Then the frightful turtle came gleefully up to the rocky beach and made a meal of the hapless ogre.

W ord of Theseus' adventures soon reached Athens. As Theseus approached the city, crowds came out to greet him.

"Who performs these daring deeds?" Aegeus asked. "Let me meet the valiant champion." Aegeus decided to honor the stranger's bravery with a magnificent banquet in the Temple of Dolphins. When the prince stepped forward to present himself, the old king recognized the sandals and the golden sword, and he knew the youth before him was his son. He welcomed Theseus with a cry of wonder and a loving embrace. The sight of their happy reunion filled everyone with joy, and the people feasted, danced, and lit altars in every temple in Athens.

One morning shortly after the festivities ended, Theseus sensed a terrible sadness throughout the city. He also saw that his father's brow was creased with sorrow.

"Across the sea, a powerful king named Minos rules the island of Crete," Aegeus explained. "He keeps a beast called the Minotaur, a monster that is half-man, half-bull and feeds on human flesh. Many years ago, Minos' son visited our city and was killed here by a bull. In his rage, Minos made war on us and threatened to destroy Athens unless we sent him a tribute of seven young men and seven young women every year to sacrifice to the Minotaur. The time has come again to pay the tribute," he finished bitterly, "and though I am their king, I can do nothing to protect the fourteen who will draw unlucky lots and be sent to Crete, never to return."

Theseus, angered by King Minos' cruelty, replied, "Let me go with those to be sacrificed. I will slay the Minotaur and end the curse that hangs over our city." Aegeus pleaded with him to stay in Athens, but Theseus remained steadfast and prepared for the voyage to Crete.

The next morning, the old king was forced to bid his son farewell.

"In mourning for those to be sacrificed," said Aegeus, "your ship has a black sail.
If the gods grant you the power to kill the Minotaur, hoist this white sail on your return.
I will see it far out on the horizon and rejoice that you are safe." Theseus promised his
father he would remember, then eagerly boarded the vessel. Many around him wept at the
sad departure, but Theseus could think only of the thrilling adventure before him.

The ship sailed south and soon approached the shores of Crete. A towering figure ran back and forth across the harbor entrance.

"What is this marvel?" cried Theseus in wonder.

"That is Talus," replied the captain. "A senseless giant made of bronze. It moves as though it were alive and guards the harbor against King Minos' enemies. He would smash us to bits if it were not for our black sail, which even he can recognize." The mechanical man allowed the Athenians to pass him as they approached the king's immense palace, where Minos and the Minotaur were waiting for them.

Not only Talus watched the ship arrive. From a bluff, Ariadne, the daughter of King Minos, stood with her friend Icarus and gazed down at the somber ship. Icarus was the son of Daedalus, a famous inventor. Long ago, at the king's command, it was Daedalus who built a labyrinth beneath the palace as a cage to hold the Minotaur.

"Who is that, who stands so tall and unafraid on the Athenian ship?" Ariadne asked. She was impressed by the stranger's confidence.

"That must be Theseus, son of Aegeus," Icarus replied. He was pleased to be able to show off his knowledge to the beautiful princess, but he wondered at her admiration of Theseus. "I have heard he freely chose to come here and face the Minotaur."

Ariadne knew very well that no one had ever escaped the circling passages and corridors of her father's enormous stone maze. Gazing at the prince, she made up her mind to save him from the king's rash cruelty. "We must go to your father and ask for his advice," she said to Icarus. "If anyone knows the secrets of the maze and can help us rescue Theseus, it is Daedalus." The bold princess was right, for the brilliant inventor revealed to her a clever plan.

That night, while the others slept, Ariadne secretly entered the king's chamber, gathered up the palace keys and Theseus' sword, and crept down to the prisoner's cell.

"Theseus," she whispered to him, "I am Ariadne. I have heard tales of your many good deeds. I can show you how to escape the labyrinth, but in return I ask that you help me to escape this island and my father, King Minos, who has grown wicked and pitiless."

Theseus agreed to help her, and so Ariadne explained Daedalus' secret. "You must secure one end of this ball of thread to the entrance of the labyrinth," she said, "and keep hold of the rest of the ball as the string unravels behind you. If you defeat the Minotaur, the thread's path will lead you back out of the labyrinth." Praying that the gods would help him, she led Theseus to the maze and watched as he descended the heavy stone steps. Then she returned to the prison hold to free the other captives.

In the corridors of the labyrinth, the odor was foul, the light dim. Theseus gripped his father's sword in one hand, and in the other he held the unraveling thread. The passages twisted and turned, leading him first one way and then another, winding around and around. Down, down he went, searching for the beast hidden deep in the black abyss.

Finally he came to an open space where the Minotaur lay sleeping on the rough stone floor. Its hot breath shook the cavern walls. The creature had the chest and arms of a powerful man, but the rest of its body had the shape of a bull, and two great horns grew out of its head.

Then the Minotaur opened one glowing red eye and fixed it on Theseus. Its snore died away, and the chamber grew deathly still.

With a thunderous bellow, the Minotaur rose to its feet and charged. Theseus leapt aside, but the deadly horns grazed his tunic. The Minotaur spun around, furious, and charged again. As the beast descended upon him, Theseus steadied himself, raised his golden sword, and with a great heave drove the blade through the Minotaur's heart. The monster dropped to the cold stone floor, silenced forever.

Shaken by the fury of the struggle, Theseus had dropped the ball of thread.
Anxious to escape the gloomy maze, he picked it up again and followed the thread out of
the labyrinth and into the cool night air.

Ariadne and Icarus were waiting for him. The princess cried out with delight to see
Theseus unharmed.

"Let us waste no time in leaving. The king is sure to come after us," urged Ariadne.
Theseus and the freed Athenians boarded the ship, but Icarus stepped back.

"Minos will blame Daedalus for your escape. I cannot abandon my father to the
king's wrath," he explained, though it pained Icarus to see Theseus leave with Ariadne.
"Daedalus and I will flee Minos together," he vowed. "Then we will join you in Athens."

Icarus watched from the bluffs as the ship set a course for Athens, but he was not the only one who followed the black sail in the breaking dawn. At the harbor entrance Talus spied the ship and raised his heavy club high to strike the boat. Theseus stepped forward with his sword, prepared to fight. But Poseidon, ever watchful, sent a massive wave smashing into the bronze giant. The Athenians watched in awe as the shining colossus, crushed into a heap of broken metal, sank to the bottom of the sea.

When King Minos woke and discovered all that had happened, he was enraged. Minos knew Daedalus was to blame for Theseus' success — for who else was clever enough to show the hero a way out of the labyrinth? To punish the inventor for his deception, the king locked both Daedalus and Icarus high up in a tower.

From a window in the tower, Icarus watched the birds and looked out to sea, imagining the fast ship that carried Ariadne and the Athenians to safety. He pictured the hero's welcome that Theseus would receive and longed for his own freedom and glory.

"Look how easily the birds move about!" he sighed to Daedalus. "It is their wings that make them free."

Now, Daedalus had a mind so wondrously quick that no one could keep it locked up. He devised a plan for escape and cunningly asked Minos for his tools and materials. The king agreed, wondering greedily what new marvel the inventor would make for him.

Then Daedalus had Icarus gather feathers from the birds that rested on the window ledge. When Icarus had piled up two great mounds of feathers, Daedalus went to work, fashioning two marvelous pairs of wings held together by threads and wax. One day Icarus and his father attached the wings to their arms and shoulders and climbed into the tower windows. As they prepared to make their daring escape, Daedalus cautioned his son.

"Take a middle course, Icarus," he warned. "If you fly too low, the sea will soak the feathers. If you fly too high, the sun will melt the wax."

Off the window ledge they launched themselves, soaring into the sunlit sky like two grand eagles.

Icarus flew up high and dove down low, skimming the waves with delight. Then he climbed back up, higher and higher, spiraling toward the sun.

"Icarus!" called his father. "Remember my warning!" But Icarus did not want to take the middle course. Reveling in his freedom, he pumped the fantastic wings through the air and watched the ocean spread beneath him like a shining jewel. The higher he flew, the more powerful he felt. He vowed he would never again be caged.

Icarus flew closer and closer to the sun. Its warmth slowly melted the wax, and feathers began to fall from his wings. Suddenly Icarus, too, was falling. "Father! Father!" he cried. But Daedalus could only watch in horror as his son plunged into the water and drowned beneath the waves.

The grieving father buried his son on an island nearby, which came to be called Icaria. Then, his heart heavy with sorrow, Daedalus flew on to the island of Sicily, where he was welcomed with honor. In spite of his sadness, the great inventor lived to create many more wonderful things. But he destroyed the fateful wings and never flew again.

Oblivious to the terrible fate of Icarus, Ariadne and Theseus stopped their ship to rest on the isle of Naxos, unaware that the god Dionysus was following them. Dionysus was the god of wine and lord over all feasting and revelry. He had fallen in love with Ariadne, and while the Athenians slept he appeared to Theseus in a dream. "You cannot take the princess with you to Athens," Dionysus declared, "for I wish to make her my wife." Now Theseus had no choice but to leave, for he knew it would be foolish to challenge so mighty a god.

When Ariadne woke and found herself alone, she felt bitterly betrayed. But Dionysus was true to his word and married Ariadne. Over time she grew to love him in return and also became a great queen. When she died, Dionysus placed her jeweled crown in the sky, forming the constellation Corona Borealis. In the night sky, you can still see its diamonds shining like distant stars.

In Athens, King Aegeus watched for his son's return. Theseus was so exhausted from his journey and troubled by his loss of Ariadne that he forgot to put up the white sail his father had given him. When Aegeus saw the ship with the black sail on the horizon, he believed Theseus was dead. Without his son, all the old king's power and his beautiful city seemed meaningless to him. Overcome with despair, Aegeus threw himself off the cliffs and perished on the rocky shore below.

When the Athenians recognized the ship entering the harbor, they raised Theseus up as their greatest hero and new king. Though Theseus had saved many victims from the Minotaur and was glorious in the eyes of his city, he despaired at his own carelessness and wept for King Aegeus' tragic death.

Theseus named the blue sea around Athens the Aegean Sea in his father's honor. He brought his mother, Aethra, to the court, and with her advice, the young king who had been a valiant but reckless champion ruled Athens with wisdom and justice.

As Poseidon looked on, the city and its people grew in fame and influence through the ages. Its storytellers never tired of weaving tales about the adventures of Theseus, Ariadne, Icarus, and all of the famous heroes and heroines, gods and goddesses, and fabulous creatures of ancient Greece.

Olympus, home of the gods

Ionian Sea

Sicily

Mediterranean Sea

Troezen

Crete

ANCIENT GREECE